The Collective Works Of Martin Dansky's Poems and Paintings

1999-2003

The printing of this book has been made possible through the kind support of these people and businesses:

Jacqueline A. Barrow
Le Baz'art, 1110 Mont Royal East
K. David Brody C.Tr.
Mrs. D. Cohene
Cafe les entretiens, 1577 Laurier East
Mr. Dency Dimanno
Galerie 1040, 1040 Marie Anne East
Mr. Jacques Gagné
Mr. and Mrs. A. Greenberg and family
Herve and Florence Lalo
Mr. Peter Lymberiou at Dusty's
Drs. L. Dansky and E. Garfinkle and family
Mr. and Mrs. S. Lazarus
Yanni Moulatsiotis
Madame Louise Pilon
Leonard Posner
Chris Powell
Jon Primiani
www.sollythecaterer.com
Mr. and Mrs. G. Susser
Mr. James W. Taylor
Mustafa Zaisi at K2 Solutions

The following pieces are poems I wrote accompanied by my artwork reflecting the mood and spirit of the written work. Enjoy.

Martin G. Dandy

Metro Crossing.....48"x40" acrylic on canvas

Metro Crossing
September 18, 2001

There is a passing in the night
ghostly images peer in on unsuspecting readers
flipping through fate filled pages.
Like mother, the daughter learns from example
and becomes the product of what she reads and where she lives.
They sit on top urban rooftops aside past legends and tales of heroism
keeping a toe-hold in the world of the concrete present
in many a private room where books are rarely opened.

There is a passing in the night
as gods from the past observe the innocent on passenger cars
lying beneath our modern cityscapes
grown out of rock filled quarries
their ghosts don't bleed
their weapons already pulled from holy sites
in magic performances they weigh our deeds
while we continue to look for unsuspecting ways to succeed.

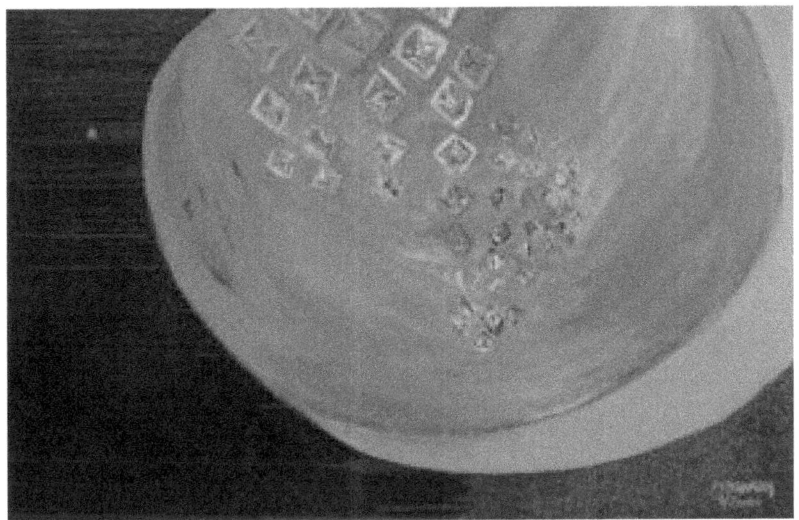

Raining Diamonds on Neptune.....48"x40" oil on acrylic

In the Bag
Aug 6, 2003

How to get to know another party
when you ask what's in the bag
as you pilfer another for a fag
to learn said company is such a drag.

A bag of lace is carried with grace
while one of leather toted by tethers
a tiny symbolic one may carry a regal seal
morc combersome ones will load with orange peels.

I live in a world of a bag for all occasions
carried from shops with determined destinations
part of an ulpan to fill cultural voids
part of a greater plan for humanoids.

Who can stuff their bags with fresh produce
who can extract a fag to then deduce...
just ask your neighbour what's in the bag
pretend you're interested, or you'll be had.

Mother Child Chase.....24"x18" oil on paper/canvas

Preventive
August 5, 2003

Suggestive of cures to halt a malady's success
preventive means to malt the brew in progress.

A lotion applied to keep the dryness away
a potion prescribed to let the pleasure stay.

Tissues ask that their essential oils remain
fixtures tasked to prevent potential strains.

Preventive conflict stikes any given day
and oppressive orders are meant to stay
if only to keep struggles in check were as much sincere,
as to accept national diversities...
come to grips with real conflicts to fear.

Trials and errors pose at regular refrains
medicinal doses quantify usual pain.

Induced by parasitic enclaves at national posts,
promoted by market racketeers or talkative hosts.

Do we live in a preventive manner
or live in substantial manor?

Is this the manor that was meant to be
or is it the manner of preventive needs?

Cup and Prayer.....24"x18" oil on canvas

Reward
July 6, 2003

Only for the lost cat on the block?
Only for the return on gained stock?
redeemed when a foreign student has spoken
where a cultural barrier has been broken.

I mean... not broken like a bottle of wine
or a broken wish, now fruitless,out of line
but a hurdle over the barrier of the spoken word
where there are often more subtler means to be heard.

A gesture of good will can n'er be overlooked
a common courtesy that comforts the crooked
makes them forget when it's time for new words to be used
an innate acquisition of associated customs should be perused.

Herald the new means of creation..brighter purpose for your words
most often there are subtler means that scratch to be heard.
sounds garnish the palate of your mouth..and form that speech
that looks towards an inevitable cultural barrier to breech.

Clown New Year.....20"x18" oil on canvas

Slow or Fast Lane
June 29, 2003

There are some who sit and watch time roll by
and others who rush around at their wit's end,
still ones that look back to clocks in retrospect
about the lives they led, the way it was spent.

Some who made their mark, left around the bend
then ones who scurried round in the fast lane
to live a wonderous life: wonder where it all went;
the mace to wield, chalice to fill,an arrow bent.

There are ones who ran around in the fast lane
who challenged a life, known not to be seen again
to live in question, how it was consumed or spent..
yet others rock gently on porches full of time on hand.

Life slipped through porch fingers again and again
it slipped out of crash victims who did not restrain
both the quick and the slow observed sunsets still
no matter who you were with father time on the till
the rebel rousers, no moment to spare on a campaign

the sedate ones, rocked easily now and then
look back in retrospect...did they all get respect?

911.....18"x12" oil on canvas

Three Strikes
June 25, 2003

Land of justice variants in different states
land of where real justice begins..eternal debate
too much of it injures the cow that feeds its young
too little of it leaves indignation among the stung

Land of the free within reason
free to express myself, vote for positive effects
not free to avoid its long term defects...
that brands the petty thief
along with his hardened relative...

Three strikes and you're out
away from the bat or any free run
but sport is different from the application of law
when a marked man reunites with society years later
there's one large flaw...

All the time he had to build a life, is gone
these years can never be replaced
yet the family of victims rightly sings a different tune,
a loved one's life can't be replaced either.
Would it just be better to leave earth for life on the moon?

Blind Valentine.....20"x16" oil on canvas

She Saw Red
June 12, 2003

She saw red
it was a bleed..
Shock at the race track
had her see the crimson leak
that kept her from a moment's rest.

An experience of a bleed back then
had her cower from a torrent of kisses;
shielded herself from unforsaken love
how unwanted...how invasive.

Whatever shock that followed
would rekindle the scarlet glow;
a crimson leak...so long gone
had sent its tentacles forward
to mar her clarity of vision
on the hunt to catch the vixen....

that same hunt that saw her horse
suffer from a head-on collision
re-enacted a childhood vision
another hunt of course.

On the run..she would still see red
until a man would have her confront
a moment in her childhood past
unearth an uncomfortable approach
another man...actually her mother's lover
of the accident..suspicions hovered
when she defended herself
against an unwarranted love.

Dragon New Year.....10"x8" oil on canvas

An Error of Love
July 13, 2003

Is it only the entitled which you entertain
and lack of class which you disdain
questions of rank or virtue or do I abstain?
Are opinions just that and nothing more
or lack of office that gentry abhors;
what of religion, color and creed
not to mention lesser misdeeds?

Of the patient who chances cures at home
as health care systems are run by gnomes,
shake the system...shake n bake
a doctor's daughter labelled fake
Of his malpractice, she is not to blame
you'd sooner choose her
had daddy come to fame.

Her family's denied access to chosen tables
doesn't exclude the fact of her being able
and the good stand tall without titles.
If it's only the nameless that you disdain
rudeness comes with names just the same
and honored bodies return to nature
whether of 'good' blood or high stature.

Since she is young fair and wise
why point out bloodlines you dispise
in common folk honor surely thrives
from which love may otherwise derive.

So love the maiden for who she is
a heavenly king will provide the rest
if it's only a title for which you abstain
question not common stature that you disdain.

Lady in The Spotlight.....14.5"x12.5" pastel on paper

Celebrity
July 29, 2003

Fortune rests in chimerical packs
polished car hoods and china stacks
tea time's arranged through a mad hatter agent
famous by deranged calls to punctual pageants.

Cued act microphone invites a speaker
back of megaphone hides the peeker
celebrity status is on the rise
let morning bird chitter arise.

Celebrities exhibit there ware for tear
stand up to the test of public scrutiny
so did pirate crews on hoisted sail mutinies
centuries before American idol worshipers cared...

So what do I say of the celebrity out there,
about pretty faces when their lives are laid bare,
about handsome traces when evolved to has beens..
as famous words step into devolved worlds we're in?

it's okay to be a "star"
if it doesn't go to your head
it's okay to fly "afar"
when you'd rather be home instead.

Sand Bag Home.....≈ 16"x12" oil on canvas

Coastal Blue
July 22, 2003

The way it is or was repeated
how darker thoughts would be defeated
a sunlit blue sky screen
conciousness of silent screams

poked through tall stalks
with the fingers of the hands
stretched and pointed...
then curled, disjointed

fingers attached to palms and wrists
the cobalt blue...seafaring hue

the way it was repeated
the ecstasy of a sky watch

touched sepals of wildflower sorts
laced a myriad of coastal ports

feast on the open face of blue
and a daytime watch for you.

Next Door Neighbour.....12"x9" pastel on paper

Love Bug
July 12, 2003

Two door car fit to rattle
shake, rattle, roll
steered through plains mounted in cattle
neck surrounded in a vixen stoles
away, away to a high heeled venue
tinted class models in park menus.

Herby and friends part of American landscape
hearts cry..for compact culture's no escape.

Away from the old, in newer car traps
two door car made to shake faithfully
raked those leaves from favorite hubcaps
beetle shielded from insect bites regularly
magic comfort airs through open tops
served generations at sacred truck stops.

compact bug culture a people's dream
laden with roof racks of chromium gleam.

Golden lime beetle charmed its riders
riders of the storm, and beach walk striders
love bug romance end is imminent
assembly lines are never permanent
two door car made for vixen stoles
made for platform shoes
gentlemen strum guitars to the muse
of automated culture off racks in the news.

Love bug once part of American venues
will there be another set on the menu?

Road to Mahweet.....11.5"x9.5" oil on canvas

Coppermine
June 1, 2003

An eloquent metallic name for a northern river
courses through tundra... exposed gentle escarpments
orangy glint through the water's surface
a source still said to be free of hazardous waste

800 people live at the river's mouth, near ice floes
who've only known the distilled taste that flows
from miles away...
but the law of land is still governed
from even further...by decision makers
and advantage takers
who turn their taps on chlorine affected editions..

A continued upset of other water traditions
now on my dismal list of latest predictions....
you see all you have to do is listen to the news
that calls for studies on how not to disturb
the tendency to destroy continues to perturb...
a continued tendency on how to be shrewd...
underestimate ecosystems for renewed exploration

The way to end lives
as one effects a water's oxygen level
cut prematurely short by chemicals
that promotes the growth of algae
that kills the fish
that ruins countless more livelihoods
and ruins the homesteads on distant river shores
pollution would be the price of progress galore!

Man in Red Suit.....12"x10" oil on canvas

The Red Jumper
June 25, 2003

This was a set made for look alikes
sisters posed one afternoon..in their made to measure outfits
little did they realize they'd outgrow the jumpers soon
from a set of red corduroy jumpers that matched
the years would fill them with fond memories of the soft fabric.

Tiny outfits were complete with pockets for a queen
as new kids on the block, the creation won esteem
see how the jumper is quickly outgrown
be it constructed from fabric carefully sewn;
the child begins to choose something else
perhaps it was the color, or the style
and the outfit begins to gain disfavor.

Popularity among garments quickly heightens...
a familiar, comfortable fit soon tightens;
still in the early years, as part of the molt,
once familiar clothes are abruptly discarded...
or stashed behind more recent acquisitions.
A garment is lost after a bout of inquisitions

This was a matching set
parents don't make the effort they used to
we've gone the synthetic way
praise be the scientific sway
that got the girls out of the clothes that matched
and set them on their separate ways that hatched

from handmade cloth constructed for pleasure
it was the matched set that was made to measure.

Abstract Study 2000.....20"x16" oil on canvas

Predation
June 22, 2003

The nature of the beast behind the bush
in wait for its inevitable dinner plate....
nature of a lull...propagated savanna hush
an expected rush succeeds a communal fate

The rush to seize..a trophy lies on hoof
a momentous freeze...foundation to roof;
eyes that glare between the blades of brush
still squint to select a victim to rush

Audiences witness this enactment for decades
stare at the rushes of the intended plate...
observe the chase from ivory mounted arcades
wait for inevitable conclusions...continued fate

That same audience is observed from somewhere
through some giant intergalactic telescope...
sees us plunder selected impoverished wares
target predestined souls..that aim nowhere.

Their outcome like that of the lame wildebeast
is a garnished plate for the savannah feast.

Greek Vase.....20"x16" oil on canvas

Tatooed Memories
June 21, 2003

Those are the ones around the nape
a gnome about to pick a fair grape
attack a maiden on an extremity
and a strongman in the midst
to keep the lethal grasp at bay.
Body shapes take form..displayed
all in black and white
the topmost of a vaster incised stock
a gallery of victims, heros.

Those around the legs
are lesser unsung heros...
the face of a mother on one sartorius
the cross for a father on a gluteus
a singer and drummer from favorite band days
the shapes take form...this is body art
add another story...where do I start?
Choice narrows down to a remote tendon
and yet some must continue
in the way of designs and signatures
no longer a blue collar identification...
a search for illustrated recognition?

Balcony Spirits.....20"x16" oil on canvas

Taxi!
June 14, 2003

Slouched in the front seat
newspaper rolled up
tossed aside
face hidden behind the visor
a taxi man called for hire.

And you tap on the backseat window
a door clicks to be opened
you would deposit your daily load
don't talk to strangers we're told
so you crease a seat...slip inside
another sees how carefully you hide....

Observed through a rear-view mirror
a slouched form stretched
ready to grasp a steering wheel...
you detect a rasp...a voice...
where will it be?
along a road..up a tree?

Now how many have indicated where to go
to find there's no real place on show
yet we set the stage for increased pace
cover blemishes with hand woven lace;
there lies a tension between a passanger of sorts
and a face behind the taxi visor in retort....

Of commands that stand the test of time
like multiply, go forth, seek and find;
to find the place for us to reach
it's a destiny from backseats we seek.

Pastel Look.....18"x12" oil on canvas

The Penny
June 22, 2003

Lonesome penny on a rug fringe
spilt from a pocket during binge
will it see the comfort of another hand
or left to accrue sediment..let to stand.

That a lucky day will still evolve
I pick up pennies with strong resolve
they lie on the ground and feel dejected
was a time when the penny was respected.

Ramadan.....12"x10" oil on canvas

Comics can Harvest Grain
September 30, 2001

It all started among a group of gods
they chose to find a comic to entertain their needs,
who would tickle their fancy
and juggle their immortal spirits.
He would throw them spheres of talent
that they would examine each one and digest their own portion..
for them he would be their mascot on earth,
a joker with a funny hat,
for us he would just be another tiller of the plains,
his harvests would forever rest on the horizon
and his body would forever rest in a box
designed in his own image..

Halloween Pick-up.....20"x16" oil on canvas

The Tear
June 24, 2003

The first trickle etched in folkloric memory
may have come with a hardy, uncontrollable laugh
some say it came out of tremendous sadness
when the heavens, upheld by a female's arched body,
whose arms and legs supported the heavenly vault
opened and rain, like tears began to fall...

The first trickle felt so subtle...
then as discontent mounted in the valleys below,
select valley women climbed the nearest summit,
joined the arched goddess in her lament
and weeped openly...
The first act of jealousy between brothers
magnified itself on grander scales
these were their men they cried for...

The first trickle then became an announcement.
Inhabitants would know of future jealous acts
cause the rain would fall, at first as tears
and rush down as daggers..then clear sheets
created torrents from dry river basins
widened their banks and deepened their beds...
the women on the crests chose to weep instead.

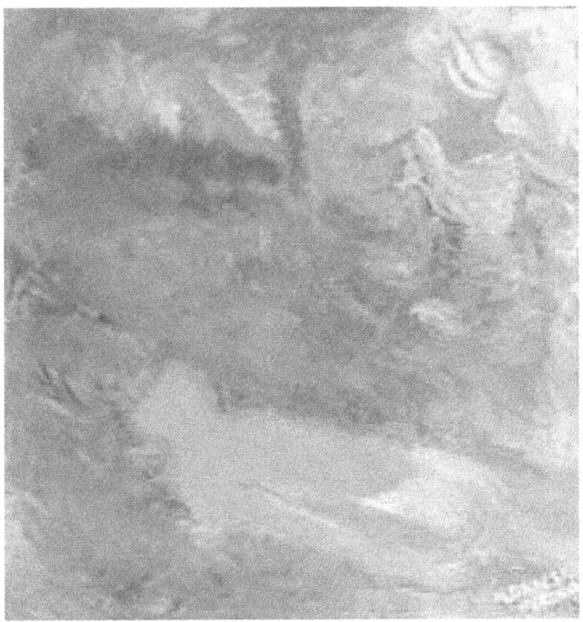

Holy Spirit.....20"x16" oil on canvas

Indian Lament
July 4, 2003

Son let me tell you
of the trains of people and their culture
of the wounded deer and the circled vulture
let me remind you
of the buffalo that had once roamed free
the faces carved from majestic Douglas trees.

Let me tell you
what our people hold true
you are the future of my proud race
vultures eat carrion...when life shows no trace
trains of people long displaced the buffalo
we used to hunt...then cultivation followed
be aware of the white man and his ways
he came to help and now he stays.

When he forced us off the land we hunted
we were directed to cultivated land salted...
with the bones of the buffalo massacred by their hands,
nothing would grow from the earth where we stand.
To remove us from the depression that then followed,
he sent us a strange religion we're forced to swallow.

Make sure before you give up any more of our forefathers' land,
find out from past experience where your future will stand.

Shelves of Experience.....18"x12" oil on canvas

Bird in a Cage
July 26, 2003

Bird in a cage
from first to second stage
little baby born..its the rage.

Worth two in the bush
we all fall down...hush
hush little baby, don't you frown
mama's got a gift...you won't drown
bird in a lift
scissor-tailed swift
hush little baby..don't cry a word
enjoy the life in lands of the absurd
follow the chant of the mockingbird.

Follow the chant of a bird that mimics
stunts of ones that call for gimmicks
of a brightly tailed parrot
that mocks you for a carrot
and a cockatoo that calls for more,
little one grown...you'll exit that door
mind you're careful not to scuff the floor
no longer a bird in a cage
announced by a residential page.

Freed from capture in the family lift
liberated scissor-tailed swift
into the air...fly far and wide
market yourself across the divide
for the ocean's a lake for some on the wing
that newborns are carried to parents in slings.

Cherish your moments in lands of the absurd
recognize the deceitful chant of the mockingbird.

Movie Spirits.....20"x16" oil on canvas

In the Mainstream
July 28, 2003

In the mainstream
fish fries hatch in still waters
the salmon takes on its classic coat
subjected to current flux like classic floats.

A show of wills..transports its masters
who will arrive, the sooner or faster
from the corners of the earth, all laden with gifts
and a star that shone bright and had me miffed.

test of skills..determined wills
ones made to sign, to ethereal designs

A moment of will, a test of strength
wake up my darlings before its too late
from the boredom that surrounds city dwellers
to the movement in traffic all helter-skelter.

Directed lives to a chosen path
remembered the initiated chosen swath,
Is it a random assortment of causes without ends
and a laisser-faire attitude that makes no amends?

Show of wills, directed skills
sharpened wits emerged from pits
in the mainstream floated on a rapid course
arguments raised till voices grow hoarse:

"who will arrive sooner or later
is diminished in size
or made much greater".

Pride Parade.....12"x10" oil on canvas

August, 2003

The missing seals
echos of harpooned hunts
spun underwater stunts

lifelessly lined on coasts
exhibit A: mysterious breadknife cut
echos of harpooned spoils
they say the ocean spray toils

"What do you make of it?" says scientist A to B?
"Greenland sharks are too far out to sea
to venture to this marooned, saltwater coast
and leave breadline cuts on seal hosts."

"Much to speculate at mysterious ocean poles," replies B
there's not much to conjecture at one fauna loss
if we stop to think that we are not in control
another point for the sea's efficient patrol
where elements of nature ruefully reign...
much to our frustration and perennial disdain."

"And we can barely ferry out to sea
in difficult times it's easier to flee
from the tales of this watery crypt
another unsolved aquatic script."

Naked Spirit/Still Life.....20"x16" oil on canvas

A Lady Friend
July 23, 2003

Some would say platonic
I choose not to define,
some could add sardonic
of the unpolite kind.

It all depends on how you express yourself
whether you're keen to exploit
it all extends on how you stack that shelf
as if a magnate from Detroit...

For if you're about to use her
she will let you know, sir
yet she has been picked and rightfully coupled
no room for petty tricks, you'd find her troubled..

Of the thoughtful kind towards domestic cats
wipe your shoes on her ample welcome mat
she embodies what is rare of a permanent friend
I will cherish this bond through the very end..

Faces on the Old Walls.....11.5"x9.5" oil on canvas

An Urban Cranny
June 27, 2003

To find out where I would fit on a Friday night
free from the shackles of a mundane job
and a manager who relishes authoritative rule
free to discover some of the flavors
literally and figuratively
always present, concealed by bigger concerns...
I discovered a Belgian import eatery..
sat on a stool to enjoy a mild roast expresso
sampled a lemon filled dark chocolate
sampled a chat with the French shop assistant
who explained the freshness of his commodity
shipped weekly directly from Belgium...
could not ignore how large chain coffee shops
a haven today for university undergrads,
eager to haunt nightly study grounds
drink water passed through coffee grounds...
mark convenient table space to spread their wares
rob the intimacy away from social intercourse
they converse with their colleagues of course!

I mean I am supposed to agree to mega buck cafes
on alternate major intersections..it's the norm
so are frat party attendances at a local dorm
but there you have a choice to frequent or attend
here you have faceless coffee with which to contend.

Green men in pots of Gold.....20"x16" oil on canvas

The Pot
June 28, 2003

If you need to laugh when you are miserable
think of the poor kid with a pot on the head
who'd rather be riding his bicycle instead
when you need relief from the inequitable.

Think of unlikely trips to a doctor's bench seat,
think of two people who'd otherwise never meet;
think of the man with a dislocated jaw
wonder if he'd broken some archaic law...
who saw the poor kid in hand with his mother
couldn't figure out all the fuss and bother;
decided to laugh at the show in the clinic
removal of the casserole was no easy picnic.

The laugh that began, difficult to restrain
caused the man an infinite amount of pain,
tears began to roll down his face
unconscious was he of repair taking place.

For no sooner was laughter in your face
that the jawbone snapped back into place;
the man rewarded the child, stood and left
the child whose pot created a forehead cleft.

Organ Donors.....24"x18" oil on canvas

Detached
July 28,2003

Detached as a leaf from a stem
stitches loosen from the bottom of a hem;
they will come to you, my boy in droves
even if you stuff your face with garlic cloves.

To be required and then sought after
to be unneeded and not looked after
are at either end of the magic stick
are contraries held by the candle wick.

The wax melts and to some degree warmth is felt
I have been so accustomed as to think it permanent,
affection is as temporary as a costume belt
fit and proper for a scene, to the next a detriment.

Partake..join a group and socialize
extend your public reach..or exorcise...
of the need to be the apple of every eye
contacts inevitably break, by and by
the feel of stitches lies in the hand of the sewer
are constantly rekindled as he grows older...
or does he become imbibed in the need to reflect
about the number of stitched years he has left.

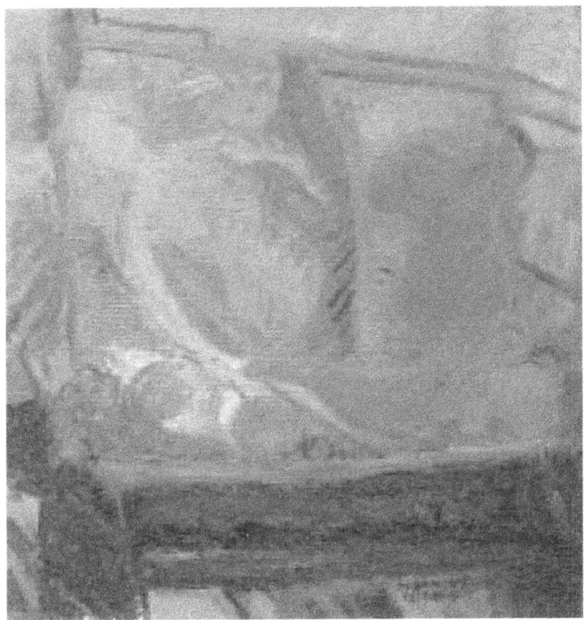

Human or Genie.....20"x16" oil on canvas

Asleep 15 years
May 31, 2003

Is it so strange to lie awake
grasp for a vision... heaven's sake
minds awake behind eye lids
the world awaits ya kid!

asleep for centuries..life has its forms
mutated through cosmic dust norms
invisible particles dance to surround sound
mind awake...yet the lids remain shut
for heaven's sake...what to make of it
take the happy ones who lace mud with straw
content with a ground meal loaf or two
grapple with the vision of a needed flute

to play for hardened sorrows to escape
so strange eyes remain open...to lie awake
peeled to a ceiling fan
to grasp ideas of new encounters

though I sailed the seas asleep for centuries
my life took to different costumes on the way
but my eyelids were difficult to open
had to manoeuvre between assorted corrective lenses

then to open a pair of eyes
there's a world I despise
yet I must continue
must sound out lonely flute notes
grasp ever pervasive encounters...
have the present slide into anonymity...

for I have slept for so many years
there came and went all those peers.

Pagoda Pumpkin.....≈12"x8" oil on canvas

Parks lead to Passages
September 18, 2003

There was an abandoned mine
in my mind
with passages that lay deep
where I learned that buried treasures lay.
I would dig daily for the truth
and hoist up treasure chests of thoughts to higher centers
but it was always nurtured by the volcanic fires within
and cooled by the surrounding ocean tides.
I had a mind full of collected fossil records
and was crowned by an old oak tree
but it was a burning desire to seek treasures in my abandoned mine
in my mind....

Spirits Behind the Trees.....36"x24" oil on canvas

From behind the Trees
September 18, 2003

There is a view from behind the trees that is safer
than the view of any conflict occurring on forest floors
in the absence of the present I'm lost in the past of cavaliers
out to protect a fair maiden's hunted choice.
Be it a fox on the run or a marmot digging away to security
we only know the chase and the victor is always up in arms
against what nature shows to have no needs.
We glorify our cause
and we remain lost in the past of chivalry, pomp and decadence
finding ourselves in a new century- the message stays the same,
Whoever dares to fight the system
creates new admirers and new enemies;
there will never be an absence of cause
only a feeling of getting lost amid the trees of our lives.

Coffee Hand.....10"x18" oil on canvas

The Ice Cream
June 10, 2003

About that flavor I never tried
that stared me in the eye
through ice cream laced windows
about choices I had to make
to make myself competitive...
those issues are repetitive
distinction on the run
exposed for summer fun?

Not really....silly.
The flavor still lies there
continually stares me in the face
even when I pick up the pace;
of the competition on the block
time to shed another frock..
confront new creamy mixtures
away from established fixtures.

A molt here..another there
need exposure to new treats
strange flavors lure;
new threats...old weapons go unsheathed
have I listened to advice?....take heed...

They stare me in the face
the years slough off...
the ice cream scoffs;
my underside remains exposed
and thin to vengeful stares;
when superficial skin is shed...
it's the future I sometimes dread.

A Brief Bibliography Of Martin Dansky

Writing:

Martin Dansky's professional writing background began in Rome in October 1996 where he contributed an article for the Avvenimenti magazine. Although he had written it in Italian he really had his heart set on writing in his own language; so when he took off to Yemen, late in 1997 he had that opportunity to do freelance for their only English language regular newspaper. He earned Yemeni wages, working for the late Dr. Saqqaf while teaching English and other subjects in the capital. Coming home a year later meant a continued search for other freelance markets, and his registering with PWAC (Periodical Writers' Association of Canada).
The Quebec Drama Federation allowed him to contribute 2 articles for their quarterly issue: he was a program co-ordinator then for the theater milieu. Today he writes for local newspapers and websites in Montreal.

Art:

Being able to identify Martin's artistic temperament through his paintings is difficult; the observer finds himself in front of paintings that are unreal or seem to have arisen from some kind of dream state. This is a special quality of the artist who likes to play with visual images and relate subtle and yet effective messages with them. There is a subtle sense of irony found in all of his paintings and these are not simple renditions of cityscapes or portrait shots. The artist incorporates psychic elements into his figurative and highly colored oil paintings. Elements of unrest and vivacity occur throughout, even in his still life sketches, the objects seem to want to skittle away. And in the turmoil of some of his dense as well as in his less crowded compositions, there is always a balance of color. The viewer is attracted to specific intricate details of the individual works while getting an overall view: generally the paintings have to be revisited more than once.
The artist has exhibited paintings since 1992 in Italy, Poland, England, the Czech Republic, Yemen, the U.S. and Canada. His 21st exhibit was at the Artus Gallery May 2003.

September 2003

www.ingramcontent.com/pod-product-compliance
Ingram Content Group UK Ltd.
Pitfield, Milton Keynes, MK11 3LW, UK
UKHW051133260726
13967UKWH00010B/3030